Is There a Thief on Bus Five?

"There's something fishy going on here," James said to Natalie. "How can our driver be so sure we'll get our missing stuff back— unless he knows where it is?"

"You don't think he took it, do you?" Nat said, wide-eyed. "I mean, Rick *is* a wild man. But I can't believe he's a thief. Besides, why would he want our junk?"

"Beats me," James said. "But *someone* on Bus Five is playing finders keepers, and I think Rick knows more about it than he's telling us."

The Kids on Bus Five

#1 The Bad News Bully

#2 Wild Man at the Wheel

#3 Finders Keepers

Available from MINSTREL Books

THE KIDS ON BUS FIVE

FINDERS KEEPERS

BY MARCIA LEONARD

Illustrated
by Julie Durrell

A MINSTREL® BOOK

Published by POCKET BOOKS
New York   London   Toronto   Sydney   Tokyo   Singapore

*Special thanks to Mrs. Dalby and the inventors at Tuscan School—
especially Laura Edelstein and Harry Kohl—and to Mr. Heisen and
the inventors at Meadow Pond School.*

—M.L.

A MINSTREL PAPERBACK *Original*

A Minstrel Book published by
POCKET BOOKS, a division of Simon & Schuster Inc.
1230 Avenue of the Americas, New York, NY 10020

ISBN: 0-671-54211-7

First Minstrel Books printing January 1997

10 9 8 7 6 5 4 3 2 1

Cover art by Julie Durrell

Printed in the U.S.A.

Chapter One

Home on the Range

Natalie Adams studied the the new books lined up on the library shelf. She liked the way they looked in their bright, shiny jackets—like presents waiting to be opened. She was sure that one of them would be perfect for her. She just had to find it.

It was Monday afternoon. As usual, the school bus had dropped off Natalie and her best friend, James Penny, at the Adamses' house. Most days they hung out together till James's mom picked him up on her way home from work. But today Mrs. Adams had taken them—and Natalie's little brother, Cody—to the library.

Natalie pulled a book from the shelf. She flipped through the pages. Then she hurried over to the table where James and Cody were sitting. "This is so great!" she said. "Look what I just found!"

James set aside the book he was reading. "What is it?" he asked.

"*Home on the Range* by Ginny Cates," said Natalie. "It's about life on a cattle ranch in New Mexico." She sat down next to him and opened her book. "Look. It tells about riding and roping and roundups—all kinds of neat stuff."

"Cool," said James.

Natalie nodded happily. "I figure if I read this book, I can learn how to be a real cowgirl, just like the author."

"Forget it!" Cody said. "You're only in third grade, Nat. And you don't have a cow—let alone a horse."

"Not *yet,*" Natalie snapped. "But I will when I grow up. So I might as well get

started now. Besides, there's stuff in here I can do without a horse or a cow."

"Oh, yeah?" said Cody. "Like what?"

"Like roping." Nat smirked at her brother. "I could use you for a cow."

"No way!" Cody said loudly.

Mrs. Adams came over to the table. "Cody, keep your voice down, please. This is a library," she said. She held up two books. "I've got what I came for. So if you kids are ready, we can go now."

They carried their choices to the checkout desk. Cody had a stack of picture books. Natalie had her ranch book and a biography of Annie Oakley. James had two mysteries and a book called *How to Care for Your Puppy*.

"What's with the puppy book?" Natalie asked. "Are you guys getting a new dog?"

"*I* want one," said James. "But my parents say we have too many pets already."

He shook his head in disgust. "Can you believe it?"

Natalie had to smile. James had two cats, three gerbils, a guinea pig, a tank full of fish, some turtles, and a big old yellow dog named Honey. For most kids that would be more than enough pets. But not for James. He really loved animals.

"You already have a dog," said Cody. "How come you want another one?"

"Honey's nice," said James. "But she's older than me, and she's really my parents' dog. I want a dog of my own—a puppy I can play with and teach tricks to and stuff."

"Puppies are fun, James. But they need lots of attention," Mrs. Adams said. "Your parents both work. You're at school most of the day. How can you take care of a puppy?"

"My parents asked me the same thing," said James. "That's why I'm taking out the book. I hope it'll have some answers."

"Hey, I've got an idea," said Natalie. "When we get home, I'll help you with your puppy problem. Then you can help me learn how to rope. Deal?"

"Deal," said James.

The four of them left the library and headed for the parking lot. Nat and James were in a hurry to reach the car. But Cody walked very slowly, looking at the ground.

"Come on, Cody," Natalie called impatiently. "What's the matter? Did you lose something?"

"No, I'm looking for money," said Cody. "Last time Mom and I were here, I found two pennies. And once I found a whole quarter."

"You're kidding," said Natalie.

"Huh-uh," said Cody. "Ask Mom."

"It's true," said Mrs. Adams. "People often drop change in parking lots. Cody's good at finding it."

"Can I look, too?" asked Nat.

"Me, too?" asked James.

"Okay," Cody said. "As long as you stay away from where *I'm* looking."

Cody was walking along the left side of the parking lot. So James took the middle, and Natalie took the right.

She scuffed through the fallen leaves with her red cowboy boots. Suddenly she spied something shiny. "A dime!" she cried, picking it up. "I found a dime."

Cody charged across the parking lot. "No fair!" he yelled. "I should have found it. Give it to me."

Natalie held the dime high. "Finders keepers," she said. "It's mine now."

Cody jumped again and again, trying to grab the dime. But he was only five and short for his age, and he couldn't reach it. "Mom!" he yelled. "Make her give it to me!"

"Sorry, Cody," said his mom. "You said Nat could look, and she found the dime on her side of the parking lot. So it's hers to keep." She opened the car door. "Come on, kids. It's time to go home."

Natalie grinned. She put the dime in her pocket. Then she and James got in the car.

Cody got in, too. "Next time *I'll* be the finder," he said angrily. He slammed the door hard.

When they got back to the house, Mrs. Adams took Cody to the kitchen for a snack. Nat and James plopped down on the living room sofa and began reading *How to Care for Your Puppy*.

There were chapters on how to choose a puppy, how to feed it, groom it, train it, and keep it healthy. But there was nothing about how to care for a puppy when you're away from home all day.

James closed the book with a deep sigh. "So much for that idea," he said glumly.

"Hey, you're not giving up, are you?" said Natalie.

James shook his head. "No way. I'll just have to find the answer somewhere else. In the meantime, do you want to try some roping?"

"Sure!" said Natalie. She handed him her ranch book. "You find the right page. I'll go get my long jump rope. I know just where it is."

She ran upstairs to her room, flung open her closet door, and reached for the rope. The hook where she always hung it was empty.

Maybe it fell off, she thought. She poked around the closet floor, scattering sneakers and old summer sandals. The rope wasn't there. She searched her room. The rope wasn't there either. Then she noticed that two other things were missing as well.

Cody! she thought. *He's done it again!* She stomped back downstairs.

"Where's the rope?" asked James.

"That's what I'd like to know," Natalie

said grimly. She burst into the kitchen, with James right behind her.

"Mom!" she yelled. "Cody took stuff from my room again, and he didn't ask first."

"Hold on a minute," said her mother. "Are you sure? What's missing?"

"My jewelry box, my kaleidoscope, and my jump rope," said Natalie. She glared at Cody, who looked away quickly.

"Cody?" said Mrs. Adams.

"Okay, okay. I borrowed some stuff," Cody said. "I'm sorry, Nat, but I really *needed* it. I *had* to have it." He flung out his arms dramatically.

"What for?" Natalie demanded.

"For my pirate game," Cody said. "I used the kaleidoscope for a spyglass and the jewelry box for treasure."

James grinned. "What about the rope? Did you use it to anchor your pirate ship?"

Cody rolled his eyes. "No, silly. I used it

to tie up my prisoners. Come on. I'll show you."

He led the way to the basement playroom. "See?" he said, pointing proudly.

Five stuffed animals sat on the floor. They were bound together with the jump rope, tied in double and triple knots.

James and Mrs. Adams burst out laughing. Natalie laughed, too, even though she was still angry.

"Well, Cody. I can see you're very good at tying knots," Mrs. Adams said. "Now let's see how good you are at *un*tying them. Then give everything back to your sister. And please, Cody, stay out of her room."

"Okay," Cody said.

"That's what you said last time," Nat growled. "This time you'd better mean it, or I really will use you for roping practice."

Chapter Two

Captain Cheesehead

The next morning, Natalie got up early and went outside to practice roping. She hadn't had much time the day before. It had taken Cody nearly an hour to undo all the knots he had tied.

She picked out a backyard fence post to use as a cow. She made a loop in the end of her rope, flung it—and missed. Hand over hand, she hauled the rope back. She threw it again and missed again. She was still throwing, and mostly missing, when James showed up half an hour later.

As usual, his mom dropped him off on her way to work. She'd done that every school day since he and Nat were in kindergarten. They ate breakfast together. Then they rode the bus together to Maple Street School.

"Hi, Nat. How's it going?" James asked.

Natalie grinned. "Let me put it this way. I'm not quite ready for the rodeo."

"You just need a little practice," James said kindly.

"Correction, *lots* of practice," Nat replied. She coiled her rope and slung it over the fence post. "Come on, let's go in. Mom made apple muffins, and if we don't watch out, Cody will eat them all."

After breakfast, Natalie, James, and Cody walked to the school bus stop at the end of the Adamses' driveway.

"Hey, I've got a riddle for you," Cody said. "Who's gray and wears glass slippers?"

"I don't know," said James. "Who?"

"Cinderelephant," Cody said gleefully.

Nat and James grinned.

"The Wild Man told me that one," Cody said. "He knows a zillion elephant jokes."

The Wild Man was the kids' nickname for Rick DeVries, Bus Five's new driver. Natalie liked Rick. But she never knew what to expect from him. He wore colorful clothes and silly hats. He sang songs and made up rhymes and talked in funny accents. He was also an artist. But he was serious about that.

Cody had time to tell four more of Rick's elephant jokes. Then Bus Five pulled up at the stop, and the doors opened wide.

The kids took one look inside and started laughing. The Wild Man had on a hat that looked like a giant wedge of Swiss cheese!

"Like my hat?" Rick said, turning his head side to side. "It's the latest fashion from Wisconsin, also known as the Dairy State."

"It's great, Rick," said Cody.

"Excuse me," Rick said in a frosty voice. "I'm not Rick today. I'm Captain Cheesehead. Now please board the aircraft. Flight Five will be taking off soon."

James saluted. "Okay, Captain Cheesehead," he said, trying to keep a straight face.

The three kids climbed on board. Cody sat up front to wait for his friend Eli Hirsch. Eli was in morning kindergarten, too, and he got on at the next stop. Nat and James sat in back, across the aisle from Celia Cruz and Melanie Renzi, two fifth graders.

"Hey, Nat. I've got something for you," said Celia. "I won it at the Fall Fun Fair. But I think you should have it."

Natalie's eyes lit up. Celia, the most popular girl at Maple Street School, wanted to give her something! "Really?" she said. "What is it?"

"Just a sec. I'll find it," Celia said. She started emptying her backpack. "Here,

Melanie. Hold my stuff, will you?"

She handed Melanie three folders, a worn paperback, a notebook, a pink pocket-size flashlight, two scrunchies, a change purse, a Band-Aid box, one sock, a pine cone, a brush, a tennis ball, and a deck of cards.

Natalie grinned. Celia always looked so perfect. It was funny that her backpack was such a mess.

James grinned, too. "Man, she's as bad as Cody," he whispered.

Natalie nodded. Cody collected and saved everything. He was a born pack rat.

Celia was still poking around in her backpack. "Here it is!" she said at last. She held up a brand-new pencil. On the end, where the eraser should have been, was a small silver pony with a soft mane and tail.

"Oh!" Nat sighed. "It's beautiful."

"I knew you'd like it," said Celia. She leaned across Melanie to hand Nat the pencil—and accidentally bumped Melanie's arm.

Crash! The notebook, the folders, the flashlight, the pine cone, and everything else Melanie was holding fell to the floor.

"Oh, no! My stuff!" Celia cried. She and Melanie bent to pick up the mess. But the tennis ball rolled out of their reach.

Without thinking, Nat got out of her seat and chased it down the aisle.

The Wild Man caught sight of her in his rear-view mirror. "Sit down, please," he called. "You must remain seated until the aircraft has come to a complete stop at the terminal."

"Sorry, Rick. I mean, sorry Captain Cheesehead," Nat said. She grabbed the ball and dashed back to her seat. Then she passed it to Celia, who passed her the pencil.

"Thank you, Celia," said Natalie. She stroked the pony's mane and tail.

"You're welcome," said Celia.

The bus stopped in front of the school.

"This is your captain speaking," said Rick. "Welcome to Maple Street School. As always, I'd like to remind you to take your personal belongings with you when you leave." He tipped his cheese hat. "Thank you for your attention, and thank you for joining me once again on Flight Five."

Natalie grinned. Rick was a wild man, no doubt about it. She and James gathered up their stuff. Then they went on into school.

Chapter Three

Brainstorming

The first thing Natalie and James noticed when they got to class was that the desks had been moved. Instead of standing in rows, they were arranged in squares of four.

"Hi, kids," said their teacher, Ms. Donovan. "You'll be sitting in groups this morning, so you can brainstorm ideas for the Invention Convention."

"All right!" said James and Nat.

The Invention Convention was a project the third graders did every year. First they each made a list of problems in their lives. Then they each chose one of those problems and made an invention to solve it.

They kept track of their work in special inventor's notebooks. And at the end of the project, they got to show off their inventions to the whole school.

Natalie and James were in a group with Warren Smiley and Kate Ziegler, who also rode Bus Five. They all got out their inventor's notebooks, and James read the directions on the first page out loud.

"Look around and think about the things you need or want to do. Then make a list of fifteen to twenty problems in your life."

Natalie ran a finger down her list. "I've thought of fifteen problems. But I'm not sure I want to choose any of them for my invention," she said.

"I've got eighteen," said James.

"I've got twenty," said Warren.

"Me, too," said Kate. "And I've already picked out which problem I want to work on."

"What is it?" asked James.

Kate read from her notebook. "'When I eat pizza, the cheese slides off and the sauce drips.'" She looked up and smiled. "I'm going to invent something that will hold a slice of pizza up while I eat it. That way, I won't get all messy."

"I think getting messy is fun," said Warren. "Now, if you want to hear a *real* problem, listen to this. 'I'm learning how to play chess. So I like to keep a board set up in my room to practice moves. But my little brother knocks it over all the time.'"

"Why don't you tell him to stay out of your room?" said Kate.

"I can't. It's his room, too," said Warren.

"Believe me, even if you didn't share with him, you couldn't keep him out," said Natalie. "Cody is always sneaking into my room and taking stuff. It's a real problem." Suddenly she sat up straight. "Hey! I can add that to my list." She picked up her pencil and started writing.

"Hmmm," said James. "I wonder what you could invent to keep Cody out of your room."

"I don't know," said Nat. "Something that would catch him in the act and scare him a little, so he'd learn a lesson."

"How about an alarm?" said Kate.

"That's it!" said Natalie. "That's what I'm going to invent. A Cody alarm."

The other kids laughed.

"I wish I could invent a Mitchell alarm for *my* little brother," said Warren. "But I guess I'll invent a way to keep the chess pieces on the board instead."

"Sounds good," said James. Then he sighed. "That takes care of everyone but me. I can't decide which problem to work on."

"Read us your list," said Kate. "Maybe we can help you choose."

"Okay," said James. He began to read. "'One, manatees in Florida are getting hurt

23

by motorboat propeller blades. Two, poachers in Africa are killing black rhinos to get their horns. Three, tamarin monkeys in Brazil are losing their habitat. Four—'"

"Wait a second," said Warren. "Is your whole list like that?"

"Pretty much," said James. "I wrote down the biggest problems I could think of."

"Maybe they're a little *too* big," Kate said gently.

"And a little too far away," Natalie added. "How about solving an animal problem that's closer to home?"

James frowned. "Like what?"

"Like your puppy problem," said Nat.

"What's that?" Warren asked.

"I want a puppy," James said. "But my parents say no, because nobody's home to feed it and walk it and keep it company during the day."

"Right," said Natalie. "But what if you

invented a machine that could do all that? What would your parents say then?"

James's face cleared. "Maybe they'd say yes," he said. "That's a great idea, Nat. I'll do it. I'll invent a puppy care machine."

"All right!" Warren said. "Everybody's picked out a problem. What do we do next?"

"We try to solve them," said Kate. She turned the page in her notebook and read out loud. "'List fifteen to twenty solutions to your problem.'"

"Whew! That's a lot," said James. "We'd better get started."

They brainstormed for fifteen minutes—until it was time for gym class. They talked again over lunch and again as they boarded Bus Five at the end of the day.

"A robot," Warren said. "That's what you should make, James, a kid-size robot with a computer for a brain. Then you could program it to take care of the puppy."

James waved at Warren. "Hello-o! Remember me, James Penny? I don't know how to program a computer any more than you do."

"Too bad," said Warren. "A robot dog walker would be so cool."

He and James took a seat together. Kate and Natalie sat across from them. Suddenly Natalie noticed something strange going on at the back of the bus. Celia Cruz was crawling down the aisle on her hands and knees!

"Celia! Are you okay?" Natalie asked.

"Uh-huh," said Celia. "I'm just looking for my flashlight. I think I lost it here this morning. Remember when all my stuff fell on the floor?"

"Sure," said Natalie. "Wait, I'll help you look." She crouched in the aisle and peered under the nearby seats.

"I'll look on my side," said James.

Warren went to check up front, and Kate

and Melanie joined the search, too. Soon there were kids crawling all over the bus.

Rick turned in his seat. "Hey! What's going on here?" he said. "You guys look like a bunch of mice in a cheese shop. Sit down, please—and don't get any funny ideas about my hat." He patted his Captain Cheesehead hat.

The kids all sat down.

"Sorry, Rick," said Celia. "They were just trying to help me find my flashlight. I think I lost it on the bus this morning."

Rick stood up and faced the kids. "Okay, let's all help Celia," he said. "When I count three, I want everything off the floor, including feet. Ready? One, two, three!"

The kids lifted their stuff and their feet. Then Celia went up and down the aisle, checking under each seat.

"Do you see anything?" asked Natalie.

"A Slinky and some colored pencils," Celia replied. "But no flashlight."

"I'm sorry, Celia," Rick said. "Maybe you left it somewhere else."

"I don't think so," said Celia. "But I'll check around school tomorrow."

"I hope you find it," said Rick. "And I hope someone claims the Slinky and pencils. To be honest, I'm getting a little tired of picking up after you kids. Please try to be more responsible with your stuff. Bus Five has become a major supplier to the lost and found."

He sat back down and started up the bus.

Twenty-five minutes later, Nat and James were at the Adamses' house. They said hello to Natalie's mom. Then they went to the kitchen to get a snack.

They were just finishing the leftover apple muffins when they heard strange noises coming from Cody's room.

"What's that?" said James.

"I don't know," said Nat. "Let's go see."

They went upstairs and peeked through Cody's open door.

Cody was sitting in a big cardboard box. It was decorated with metal pie tins, cut-out stars, and paper cups. Four antennas were taped to the sides. Two more were attached to Cody's hat—along with a pink flashlight and more cut-out stars.

He was so involved in his game, he didn't notice Natalie and James. "Star Man to base," he said. "I've just blown up two bad-guy space invaders. Now I'm going after another one." He made sounds like a rocket taking off, then a series of big explosions.

Nat covered her mouth so Cody wouldn't hear her laughing. Then suddenly her eyes narrowed. "Hey, wait a minute," she said. "Cody's been in my room again. That's my watch he's got fastened to his box."

"Even worse," said James, "that's Celia's flashlight he's got fastened to his hat."

Chapter Four

Finders Keepers

Natalie and James marched into Cody's room. "You're in big trouble, Cody Adams," Natalie said loudly.

Cody was so startled, he nearly jumped out of his spaceship. "Nat! You scared me," he squeaked. "You shouldn't sneak up on people like that. And what do you mean, I'm in big trouble? I didn't do anything."

Natalie put her hands on her hips and glared at him. "Oh, no? Then where did you get the flashlight? And what's my watch doing on this box thing of yours?" She nudged the box with her toe.

Cody glared back at her. "For your

information, this is a spaceship, not a box thing. It can travel anywhere in the universe, and—"

"Forget the spaceship!" Natalie yelled. "What about the other stuff?"

"Um...well...I guess I borrowed the watch from your room," Cody said in a small voice. "I needed it for my instrument panel."

"And the flashlight?" said James. "Where did you get that?"

Cody seemed relieved at the change of subject. He took off his hat and patted the little pink flashlight. "You mean this one? I found it on the bus on the way home from school. Isn't it neat?"

"Uh-huh," said James. "But you can't keep it, Cody. It doesn't belong to you."

"It does now," said Cody. "Finders keepers, remember? Just like that dime you found, Natalie."

"That was different," said Natalie. "Dimes

all look alike. We don't know who lost that certain one, and there was no way we could find out. Probably a zillion people walk through that parking lot every day."

"But we *do* know who lost the flashlight," James went on. "And even if we didn't, we could find out by asking all the kids on the bus. One of them had to have lost it."

"Who *did* lose it?" Cody asked.

"Celia Cruz," said Nat. "It fell on the floor on the way to school. But she didn't miss it till later."

James nodded. "Everyone was helping her look for it on the ride home."

"Oh," Cody said softly. He looked down. "So I have to give it back?"

James nodded. "Think about it, Cody. How would you feel if you lost one of your superhero action figures on the bus and someone found it and kept it?"

"Bad," said Cody. He took a deep

33

breath. "Okay. I'll give it back to her tomorrow."

"Good. That's the right thing to do," Natalie said. Then she put her face close to Cody's and stared into his eyes. "Now give me back my watch. And for the ninety-ninth time, stay out of my room and keep your hands off my stuff—unless I say it's okay."

Cody untied the strings that held the watch in place. "All right, already. You don't have to be so crabby about it."

Natalie just rolled her eyes. She took the watch from Cody and put it in her room. Then she and James went back to the kitchen.

"You know what?" she said. "I bet I could tell Cody a million times to stay out of my room, and he'd *still* go in there."

"I know," said James. "But I don't think he does it on purpose. He gets into one of his games, and he forgets that your room is off limits."

"Then I'd better hurry up and invent that Cody alarm to help him remember," said Nat.

The next morning, Natalie got up early to practice roping again. It didn't go much better than it had the day before. But throwing the rope and hauling it back did give her some quiet time to think about her invention.

She thought and thought, and finally she had a rough idea of how to build the alarm. The minute James arrived, she started telling him about it.

"Guess what?" she said. "I've figured out my invention. First I record a bunch of really loud sounds on a cassette tape. Bells ringing, whistles blowing, maybe a siren going off..."

"Cool," said James. "Can I help? I could record Honey barking for you."

"That would be great," said Nat. "Once the tape is made, I'll put it in the cassette player in my room, all ready to go. Then when Cody sneaks in, the player will click on, the tape will start playing, and—"

"Crash, bang, boom! Cody will get blasted by the noise," put in James.

"Right," Natalie said. "Then he'll go 'Eeeeeek!' and jump three feet in the air. And he'll run out of my room and never, ever mess with my stuff again."

James laughed. "It's terrific, Nat. But there's one thing I don't get. What makes the player click on when Cody sneaks into your room?"

"Who knows?" Nat said cheerfully. "I haven't figured that part out yet. But I will."

She and James went inside for breakfast. A few minutes later, Cody came downstairs and joined them.

For a moment, Natalie felt weird and kind of mean. Here she was, secretly planning to scare her little brother, and he didn't have a clue what was coming.

Then she remembered how many times he'd gone into her room and taken her stuff, and she got mad all over again. It would be Cody's own fault if he set off the alarm. She only hoped it would teach him a lesson.

After breakfast Cody put the flashlight in his jacket pocket. Then the three kids walked down the drive together.

As they waited for Bus Five, Cody shifted nervously from one foot to the other. "What should I say to Celia?" he asked. "She's a big kid, and I don't even know her."

"Don't worry. She's nice," said Natalie.

"Just tell her you found the flashlight," said James. "Then say that you didn't know who it belonged to till we told you."

"It's the truth," said Natalie. "Or part of it, anyway. You don't have to tell her the finders keepers part."

"Good," said Cody. Then Bus Five

pulled up at the stop, and he and Nat and James climbed on board.

"Hi, kids," said the Wild Man. As usual, he had on brightly colored clothes. But for once his head was bare.

"Hey, Captain. Where's your cheese hat?" James asked.

"At home in the fridge," Rick said. He gave the kids a toothy grin. "Sorry to look so boring today. I'm working on an idea for a new piece of art, and my head needs breathing room."

"What kind of art?" Natalie asked.

"I'm not sure yet," Rick said. "But I promise to show it to you when it's done."

"Great!" Natalie said. She turned to walk down the aisle, but Cody was in her way. He seemed to be frozen in place.

"Move, Cody," she whispered. "Celia's sitting in back. Go give her the flashlight. I'll be right behind you."

Cody sighed and started down the aisle.

His right hand was in his pocket, clutching the flashlight. His eyes were on Celia. So he didn't notice Warren's backpack sticking out into the aisle.

"Look out, Cody," called Nat. But it was too late. Cody tripped over the backpack.

Down he went, putting out his hands to break his fall. As he hit the floor, the flashlight flew from his fist. It rolled straight down the aisle and stopped at Celia's feet.

She picked it up. Then everyone started talking at once.

"Hey! It's the missing flashlight."

"Cody had Celia's flashlight."

"He took it! Cody took it."

"Cody Adams stole Celia's flashlight!"

Chapter Five

Lost and Found

Natalie and James helped Cody up from the floor. "Are you all right?" she asked.

"I'm okay," Cody said. Then his eyes filled with tears and his lower lip trembled. "Did you hear what they said, Nat? They said I stole Celia's flashlight. But I didn't. Not really. I didn't know it was hers."

"Of course you didn't," Nat said loudly. She scowled at the other kids. It was okay for *her* to criticize Cody. But nobody else had better say anything bad about him.

"Cody found the flashlight after morning kindergarten," James added. "He didn't know whose it was till we got home at the

41

end of the school day and told him."

Cody nodded hard. "I was going to give it back to you, Celia. Only I fell first."

Celia smiled at him. "Thanks, Cody," she said. "I'm sorry you fell. But I'm glad you found my flashlight for me." She turned it on. "Look, it works fine. No harm done."

"Oh, good," said Natalie. "Thanks, Celia."

She and Cody took a seat together. James sat behind them with a fourth grader named Jamal Dixon.

James leaned forward. "Whew!" he said in Nat's ear. "That's over with."

"I'm not so sure," said Natalie. She could tell that Cody was still upset. She could also tell that kids were whispering about him behind their hands. That wasn't good. She didn't want people giving Cody funny looks and making him feel bad.

Natalie was so caught up in her thoughts, it was a few minutes before she noticed something odd. The bus wasn't moving.

What's holding us up? she wondered. She craned her neck to see out the front window. There wasn't a car in sight. Rick was just staring off into space.

The kids on Bus Five began to get restless. Three second graders named Hannah, Anna, and Janna bounced up and down in the seat they shared.

"Why aren't we moving?" asked Hannah.

"I think the bus is broken," said Anna.

"I think *Rick* is broken," said Janna.

Jamal stood up and waved. "Hey, Rick!" he called. "Are we going to school or not?"

Rick gave a start. "Sorry, kids! I was thinking about my art," he said. "I guess I gave my head a little too much breathing room. I'd better wear a hat again tomorrow."

A moment later, Bus Five was on its way.

At the next stop, Cody's friend Eli got on and sat in front of Nat and Cody. Then, at the last stop before school, Hank Martin boarded the bus and joined Eli.

Hank was a fifth grader and big for his age. In the past he'd picked on anyone younger and smaller than he was. But this year he'd changed. He'd even made friends with Cody, who was the youngest and smallest kid on the bus.

Eli and Hank tried to get Cody to tell some elephant jokes. But he didn't seem interested. Finally Hank said, "What's wrong, Cody? Is something bothering you?"

Cody nodded. In a small voice he told them about Celia's flashlight.

Hank scowled. "Who was it?" he demanded. "Who's the jerk that called you a thief?" He looked around the bus, as if searching for a guilty face.

Jamal raised both hands. "Hey! Don't look at me. *I* didn't say it," he protested.

"But you've got to admit, things do have a strange way of disappearing from this bus."

"What do you mean?" Hank asked.

"Well, last week I accidentally left my baseball cap on the bus," Jamal said. "I figured it would still be here at the end of the day. But it wasn't. It was gone."

"That is strange," said James.

"I lost a minicar the same way," said Eli.

"I lost a red sweater," said Melanie.

"I lost a snake," said Warren.

"What?" cried the other kids.

Warren laughed. "A *plastic* snake. I was bringing it in to show Ms. Donovan."

"I lost a hair ribbon once," said Hannah.

"Me, too," said Anna.

"Me, three," said Janna. "But maybe not on the bus."

Other kids started chiming in.

"Wait a second," said Natalie. "I'm going to write all this down." She took out a piece of paper and her new pony pencil. Then

45

she made a list of everything that had been lost on Bus Five.

"Now what?" asked James.

"Now we try to figure out what happened to all this stuff," said Nat.

"Don't you mean, 'Now we try to figure out who took it'?" said Jamal.

"No, I don't," Natalie snapped. "I can't believe there's a thief on this bus."

"I hope you're right," said Jamal.

Bus Five pulled up in front of Maple Street School, and the kids got off. Nat put an arm around Cody's shoulders. "Are you okay now? Or do you want me to walk you to kindergarten?"

"I'm okay," Cody said softly. "Only please hurry up and find the missing stuff. That way no one can say I'm a thief anymore."

"We will," Nat said.

Cody ran off to join Eli, and Natalie and James went on to class. "That's a pretty big promise *we* made," James said. "Any idea where *we* are going to find the stuff?"

"Sure," said Nat. "Don't you remember what the Wild Man said yesterday? Bus Five is a major supplier to the lost and found. I bet he's been collecting the stuff and taking it there. So that's where we'll look first. We can skip recess and go right after lunch."

"Skip recess? I knew there'd be a catch," James said. "In that case, let's get Warren and Kate to help. The job will go faster."

At lunchtime, the four kids ate quickly. Then they went to the office and told the principal, Dr. Ives, what they wanted to do.

"Excellent," she said. "You'd be surprised how few kids actually try to track down the things they lose. The lost-and-found closet is always full."

She opened the closet door. Inside were big bins full of jackets, hats, sweaters, toys, lunch boxes, books, notebooks, and other stuff—all jumbled together.

"Yuck! What a mess," said Warren.

"I thought you liked mess," said Kate.

"Not this kind," said Warren. "It'll take years to dig through this junk."

"Good luck," said Dr. Ives, and she left them to it.

Natalie stared at the overflowing bins. "I don't even know where to start," she said.

"No problem," Kate said. "First we'll separate the stuff. Clothes in one pile, toys in another, school stuff in another. Then we'll go through the piles and look for the things on your list."

"I'll do the toys," Warren said quickly.

"Fine," said Kate. "I'll do the school stuff. Nat and James, you do the clothes. There are more of them than anything else."

Natalie blinked in surprise. Usually Kate was quiet and shy. Now suddenly she was acting like a general organizing her troops.

I bet her homework's always neat and her clothes are arranged by color, Nat thought. But a little while later, she had to admit that Kate's system worked. They'd found Jamal's cap, Eli's minicar, and most of the other stuff on the list. The only problem was, Warren kept playing with the toys.

Finally they were finished. They showed Dr. Ives what they had done.

"Marvelous!" she exclaimed. "Thanks to you, children will be able to find their belongings much more easily. How would you like to do this on a regular basis?"

"Sure," said Kate.

"No thanks," said Nat and James.

Warren just groaned.

Dr. Ives laughed. She gave them a bag for the things they had found. Then at the end of the day, James carried it onto Bus Five.

"Missing stuff! Get your missing stuff here," he called like a popcorn seller at a baseball game.

The kids gathered around, and Nat and

James gave them back their belongings.

"My sweater!" cried Melanie. "Thanks, you guys. Where did you find it?"

"In the lost and found," said Warren.

"You're kidding. I checked there," said Melanie. "But the place was a mess, and I couldn't find my sweater anywhere."

"That's because you didn't have Kate to help you," said Natalie.

Kate blushed with pleasure.

James handed Jamal his hat. "Here," he said. "Admit it. You were wrong. No one's been stealing things from Bus Five."

"Did you find *all* the stuff?" asked Jamal.

"All but the hair ribbons, some markers, and Celia's other sock," said Nat.

"That's good enough for me," said Jamal. "Okay. I was wrong—and I'm glad."

Natalie smiled. She felt as if she'd hit a home run with the bases loaded. She couldn't wait to tell Cody that the lost stuff had been found.

Chapter Six

The Cody Alarm

The next two days went by quickly for Natalie. Each morning before breakfast, she practiced roping. Each afternoon after school, she and James worked on their inventions. They even got together over the weekend to brainstorm and plan and build.

Early on, they decided to tell their families about the Invention Convention— but not what they were working on. James wanted his puppy care machine to be perfect before he showed it to his parents. And Natalie wanted to keep her alarm a surprise—just in case Cody hadn't learned his lesson.

The following Wednesday, Natalie got up early as usual—not to practice roping, but to set up the Cody alarm. She took out the special tape she'd recorded and put it in the tape player. Then she turned the volume up. If Cody sneaked into her room, he'd get an earful. She and James had recorded every loud noise they could think of, including his dad's car alarm.

The play button was on top of the tape player. Natalie stuck a stiff, square piece of modeling clay on top of the button. She stuck a plastic cereal bowl on top of the clay. Then she set the whole thing on the floor, about two feet from her bedroom door.

So far, so good, she thought. *Now for the tricky part.*

She got out some blocks and a bag of marbles. Between the door and the tape player, she built a tower of blocks. Then she carefully set the marble bag on top.

She backed away. Now if Cody opened the door far enough, he'd knock down the tower. The bag of marbles would drop into the cereal bowl, pushing down the play button. And the alarm would go off.

Natalie grinned, picturing Cody's face as noise filled the room. She and James had tried out the alarm the day before, without the tape in the player. This was going to be the real thing, the true test.

She opened her door as little as possible, slipped into the hall, and went downstairs. Her parents were in the kitchen, eating breakfast, but she went on outside. She still had time to practice roping.

Ten minutes later, James arrived. He hopped out of his mom's car just as Natalie neatly roped the fence post.

"Wow! You're getting good," he said.

"Thanks, but a fence post isn't exactly a cow," Natalie said. "I need to practice on something that moves." She grinned at

James. "How about helping me out?"

"Do I look like a cow?" James asked. "Wait, don't answer that."

Natalie laughed. "Okay, I'll ask you a question instead. How's the puppy care machine coming along?"

"Almost done. It'll be ready for the Invention Convention tomorrow," James said. "How about you? Did you set up the alarm?"

"Uh-huh," Natalie said. "Now the funny thing is, I hope Cody *does* go into my room. I want him to set it off."

"Oh, he will," James said. "I just hope we're around when it happens. It would be so cool to see the alarm work for real."

"Not to mention hear it!" Natalie said. Then they went inside.

During breakfast, Natalie kept sneaking peeks at Cody, as if he might suddenly run upstairs and set off the alarm. Luckily, he was too busy eating waffles to notice.

Afterward, the three kids walked to the bus stop. When the bus came, they said hello to Rick, who was wearing his cheesehead hat again. Cody took a seat with a second grader named named Dylan Mahoney, and James and Nat found a place in front of Warren and Kate.

"Hi, guys," Warren said. "How did you like the math homework Ms. Donovan gave us?"

Natalie clapped her hands to her cheeks. "Ahhhgh!" she cried. "Math!"

James frowned. "Come on, Nat. It wasn't that bad. Besides, you're good at math."

"I didn't mean, 'Ahhhgh, I hate math,'" Natalie said. "I meant, 'Ahhhgh, I forgot to do the homework.'"

Kate looked at her watch. "Can you do it now? You've got about twenty-five minutes."

"I can try," said Natalie. She took out a notebook, the homework sheet, and her pony pencil. Then she set to work.

Bus Five stopped for Eli and for Hank.
Then it headed for Maple Street School.

Kate checked her watch. "Ten minutes,"
she said. "How are you doing?"

"One row of problems left," Natalie said.

"Go, Nat!" Warren said.

"You can do it," James said.

Numbers buzzed in Natalie's head like
bees trapped in a hive. But she kept
working till Bus Five stopped in front of the
school.

"Two problems left!" she wailed.

"Don't stop," said James. "We'll wait for
you." He and Warren and Kate stayed in
their seats. Everyone else got off the bus.

"Come on, kids," called Rick. "Last one
to class is a rotten egghead."

Natalie slapped down her pencil and
threw up her arms like a gymnast. "Done!"
she cried. "I finished them all."

The other kids cheered. Then they all

grabbed their stuff and raced to class.

They weren't even late.

With a sigh of relief, Nat took her seat. It wasn't until later that she realized she'd left her pony pencil on the bus.

That afternoon went by in a blur. Half the time Natalie spent worrying about her pencil. The other half she spent wondering if Cody had set off the alarm.

Finally the dismissal bell rang. Without waiting for James, Natalie ran outside to the bus. She climbed on board and went straight to the place where she'd been sitting.

Her pony pencil wasn't in the seat. It wasn't on the floor or anywhere nearby.

James showed up with the other riders. "What's going on?" he asked. "How come you took off so fast?"

"I wanted to find my pony pencil," Nat said miserably. "I left it on the bus this morning. But now it's not here."

"Maybe it's in the lost and found," said Melanie.

"I doubt it," said Celia. "I left an old sweatshirt on the bus the other day. Since then, I've checked the lost and found twice. But no luck."

"Same here," said Dylan. "Only I lost my Cub Scout neckerchief."

"I lost a mystery book," said Kate.

"I lost a barrette," said Hannah.

"Me, too," said Anna.

"Me, three," said Janna. "But—"

"Hold it!" James put up both hands. "Haven't we been though this before?"

"You're right," said Natalie, "and I bet the solution is the same as before, too." She marched to the front of the bus. "Excuse me," she said to Rick. "Have you taken anything to the lost and found recently?"

"Nope, not since Monday last week," said Rick. "Frankly, I got tired of making the trip, and you kids don't seem to care much about your belongings anyway."

"*I* care," said Natalie. "The pencil I lost is my favorite."

"Oh," said Rick. He looked away for a moment. Then he turned back. "I wouldn't be surprised if you find it very soon," he said. "Maybe even tomorrow."

"You really think so?" Nat said.

"I'm sure of it," Rick said. He raised his voice. "I'm sure *all* of you will find your belongings soon. Now sit down, please. Flight Five has been cleared for takeoff."

Everyone sat down.

James nudged Natalie. "You know, there's something fishy going on here. How can Rick be so sure we'll get our stuff back—unless he knows where it is?"

"You don't think he took it, do you?" Nat said, wide-eyed. "I mean, he *is* a wild man. But I can't believe he's a thief. Besides, why would he want our junk?"

"Beats me," James said. "But *someone* on

Bus Five is playing finders keepers, and I think Rick knows more about it than he's telling us."

When they got off at their stop, Nat suddenly grabbed James's arm. "The Cody alarm—I almost forgot!" she cried.

They raced for the house.

Mrs. Adams was in the front yard, raking leaves. "Mom—where's—Cody?" Nat panted.

"He's upstairs, playing with Eli," said her mom. "How was school today, kids?"

But Nat and James had already gone inside. They were halfway up the stairs when the Cody alarm went off. Bells rang, a dog barked, pan lids clashed, a car alarm screeched and whooped.

The two of them froze, their hands over their ears. The noise was very, very loud. The strange thing was, it seemed to be coming from Cody's room instead of Nat's.

Chapter Seven

The Invention Convention

The noise stopped as suddenly as it had started. Then Natalie and James heard Cody's voice. "Let's play it again, Eli," he said. "This tape is so cool."

Nat and James took the rest of the stairs two at a time. They burst into Cody's room just as the noise began again. *Crash! Bang! Boom!* It was even louder than before.

"Turn that thing off!" Natalie shouted.

"What?" Cody shouted back. "Talk louder, Nat. I can't hear you."

With an angry cry, Natalie pounced on Cody's little tape player. She ejected the tape and waved it under his nose. "Do

63

you know what this is?" she demanded.

"Sure," said Cody. "It's sound effects for some game you've been playing."

Natalie groaned. "Yeah, a game called 'Try to Keep Your Pesky Little Brother Out of Your Room,'" she said. "Which I lost."

"Huh?" said Cody. "I don't get it."

"Me, either," said Eli.

"Let me explain," said James. "When you went into Nat's room, you saw the blocks and marbles and the tape player, right?"

"Right," said Cody. He smiled at his sister. "That's a really neat no-hands way to turn on a tape, Nat."

Natalie groaned again.

"It's more than that," James said quickly. "The whole setup—including the tape—is an alarm Nat made for the Invention Convention. It was supposed to keep you out of her room."

"Didn't the noise scare you at all?" Natalie demanded. "Didn't you jump three feet in the air and run away fast?"

Cody looked surprised. "No," he said.

"We thought it was great," Eli said.

"That's why we borrowed it," Cody said. "We wanted it for our Space Man game."

Natalie rolled her eyes. "That's it. I give up," she said. "First you take stuff from my room without asking. Then when I make an alarm to stop you, you take that, too. I might as well put a sign on my door that says, 'Help yourself, Cody.'"

"I can't read yet," Cody reminded her.

"That's not the point!" Natalie yelled.

Cody hung his head. "I'm sorry, Nat. You're really mad, aren't you?"

"Mad? Why should I be mad?" Natalie said. "You won't leave my stuff alone. My invention is a big flop. And I lost my special pony pencil on the bus. All in all, it's been a *great* day."

She turned and stomped out of the room. James went after her and tried to talk to her. But she was too upset to listen.

The next day was a half day at school. But that didn't make Nat feel better. She dragged herself out of bed. Then after breakfast she packed the alarm in a box, and she and Cody walked to the bus stop. James wasn't with them. The puppy care machine was too big for him to carry. So his dad was driving him to school.

Natalie waited for the bus in silence. She was still mad at Cody. She was dreading the Invention Convention. And she was worried about James. What would his parents think of his invention? Would they let him have the puppy he wanted so badly?

Bus Five arrived, and Nat and Cody climbed on board. Suddenly Rick started to sing. "Oh, what a beautiful morning. Oh, what a beautiful day. If you can all be patient, you'll see something special today."

Natalie felt a tickle of hope. Did Rick mean they'd find their missing stuff?

"What is it, Rick?" Cody asked.

"Wait and see," Rick replied. "All will be revealed on the bus ride home."

Natalie smiled. The Wild Man was up to something. Maybe the day wouldn't be a total loss after all.

When Nat got to school, she went straight to the cafeteria, where the third graders were setting up their inventions. James was already there, at a table across the room.

"James!" she cried, hurrying to join him. "What did your parents say? What did they think of your invention?"

James grinned. "They said yes, Nat! They said I could have a puppy."

Natalie jumped up and down. "Oh, James! That's fantastic! Tell me everything."

"Well, first of all, they couldn't believe I'd kept such a big secret," James said. "Then they said how proud they were of me and what a great job I'd done."

"You *did* do a great job," Natalie said.

James had used Honey's old wire dog cage to make a house for the puppy. He'd put a soft blanket and chew toys on the floor. He'd fastened brushes around the doorway, so the puppy could groom itself going in and out. And he'd rigged up containers that would release food and water when the puppy pressed a bar.

"I told my parents Honey could keep the puppy company while I was at school. And if we put in a dog door, it could go out in the fenced-in backyard," James went on. "That's when they said okay. I'd proved how serious I was, and I could have the puppy."

"That is so great, James," said Natalie.

Just then Ms. Donovan came by. "Five minutes till the convention begins," she called out. "Is everyone ready?"

Natalie sighed. She unpacked the Cody alarm and arranged it on the table. But her tummy filled with butterflies at the thought of showing it to anyone.

A few minutes later, the fourth graders filed into the cafeteria and started making the rounds of the tables. Natalie waited anxiously while her classmates took turns demonstrating their inventions.

One had made a ski scooter—a little wheeled cart to carry her skis. Another had made a soda can holder to store soft drinks in the fridge. Kate showed the pizza shovel she'd made by molding a piece of plastic into the shape of a pizza slice. And Warren showed his no-spill chess set, a board and pieces that stuck together with Velcro.

Natalie was next in line. The butterflies in her tummy suddenly turned into a herd of elephants wearing ten-ton boots.

"My invention is called the Cody alarm," she said. "It's named after my brother, who sneaks into my room and takes things without asking. If you have a brother or sister, maybe you have this problem, too."

Lots of kids nodded, and Nat's tummy began to calm down. She explained how she'd set up the tape player and how she'd built the block tower just behind her bedroom door.

"Now pretend my hand is the door," she said. She knocked over the blocks, the bag of marbles dropped into the cereal bowl, and the tape player clicked on. Instantly, the cafeteria was filled with loud noise.

All over the room, people reacted. Some jumped in surprise, some backed away, some covered their ears. Natalie turned off the tape. There was a moment of shocked silence. Then everyone started talking.

"Man, that scared me! It was so loud."

"It would keep *me* out of your room."

"What a cool invention! Will you help me make one?"

"Me, too. My sister's just like Cody."

Natalie smiled.

For the next two hours, different classes toured the convention. Nat set off the alarm for each new group, and each time she got a great reaction. By the end of the morning, she felt much better. Her invention wasn't a flop after all! True, it hadn't scared Cody. But if her mom had been in the house—and in on the secret—she would have heard the alarm and stopped Cody cold.

I'll tell her about it the minute I get home, Nat decided.

The dismissal bell rang at twelve-thirty. James was leaving his invention at school till his dad could pick it up. So he went with Nat to meet Bus Five.

Cody and Eli were already there, along with some other kids. But Rick waited till all the riders arrived before he opened the doors. "I promised you something special," he said. "And here it is—my brand-new work, which I call *Lost and Found.*"

The kids crowded onto the bus. There,

sitting in the last seat, was a life-size soft sculpture of a girl. She was wearing odd, mismatched clothes and three different barrettes. Next to her was an open backpack. Its contents had spilled across the seat and onto the floor. But the girl was too busy reading a mystery book to notice.

The scene was so real and so funny, everyone laughed. Then suddenly Nat spied something familiar. "Hey! That's my pony pencil on the seat," she said, pointing.

"And that's my mystery," said Kate.

"She's wearing my sweatshirt," said Celia.

"And my neckerchief," said Dylan.

James stared at Rick. "You're the one who's been taking our stuff," he said.

"Yes, but only for the last week or so," Rick said. "First I tried reminding you to take your belongings with you. Then I tried turning them in to the lost and found. When you *still* didn't seem to get the message, I decided to transform them into art."

"You mean you're going to keep them?" Nat asked in a squeaky voice.

"Of course not," Rick said. "The piece is called *Lost and Found*, not *Finders Keepers*. I made it to show you how important it is to take care of your things—and to respect other people's things." He paused and looked around the group. "Do you all understand that now? Really and truly?"

The kids nodded seriously.

"Good," Rick said. "Then let's take this baby apart."

Nat blinked. "You won't mind?"

"Nope," said Rick. "Some of the best art is temporary. Besides, I figure we can dress the sculpture in other clothes and keep it as our mascot."

He picked up Nat's pony pencil and handed it to her with a bow. "Good idea?" he said.

"Great idea," said Natalie.

Chapter Eight

Moo!

Natalie didn't see much of Cody after lunch. He went up to his room, and she and James went outside. First they played catch. Then he climbed a tree and she practiced roping. But the fence post wasn't a challenge anymore. She was just about to quit for the day when Cody came out dragging a big box. He stopped in front of her.

"What's this?" Natalie asked.

"Stuff that belongs to you," Cody said. "I went through my room and found everything I ever borrowed. Now I'm giving it back."

If Cody hadn't looked so serious, Natalie would've laughed. The box was full of odds and ends and old toys she hadn't seen in years. Most of the stuff was worn and useless. Some she even remembered giving him, like her old plastic T-ball set.

"Why are you doing this?" she asked.

Cody looked down. "Because of the Cody alarm and because of what the Wild Man said. I'm really sorry, Nat. I won't take your stuff ever again. And to prove I mean it, I'll even let you try to rope me."

"You will?" said Nat. "You'll really be my cow?"

"Moooo," said Cody.

James laughed. "I'll probably be sorry I said this. But if Cody can do it, so can I."

He and Cody took off mooing and running. Natalie ran after them. She was laughing so hard, she could barely swing her rope. But before the afternoon was over, she'd caught them both.